Sheltie☆™

and the Runaway

Written and illustrated by **Peter Clover**

ALADDIN PAPERBACKS

New York   London   Toronto   Sydney   Singapore

First Aladdin Paperbacks edition July 2000

Text copyright © 1996 by Working Partners, Limited
Illustrations copyright © 1996 by Peter Clover
First published 1996 by Penguin Books Limited U.K.
Created by Working Partners, Limited

ALADDIN PAPERBACKS
An imprint of Simon & Schuster
Children's Publishing Division
1230 Avenue of the Americas
New York, NY 10020

SHELTIE is a trademark owned
by Working Partners, Limited.
All rights reserved, including the right of reproduction in
whole or in part in any form.
The text for this book was set in Sabon.
Printed and bound in the United States of America
2 4 6 8 10 9 7 5 3 1

Library of Congress Cataloging-in-Publication Data
Clover, Peter.
Sheltie and the runaway / written and illustrated by Peter
Clover. — 1st Aladdin Paperbacks ed.
p. cm. — (Sheltie ; #3)
Summary: When a family with a girl her age moves into
nearby Fox Hall Manor, Emma hopes to make a new friend,
but the girl's overprotective father blames Emma and her
pony when his daughter runs away.
ISBN 0-689-83576-0
[1. Ponies—Fiction. 2. Runaways—Fiction. 3. Fathers and
daughters—Fiction.] I. Title.
PZ7.C62475Sh 2000
[Fic]—dc21 99-087886

Sheltie

and the Runaway

⭐ Chapter One

Emma was in the paddock trying to plait Sheltie's tail into a neat, tidy braid. Sheltie was trying to pinch the carrot that was sticking out of Emma's jacket pocket. After a lot of giggling from Emma and loud snorting from Sheltie, the little Shetland pony came out as the winner.

With a toss of his head, Sheltie galloped

off in a mad dash around the paddock. The carrot dangled from his mouth and his eyes shined, full of fun and mischief, beneath his long bangs.

"Sheltie, come back here!" Emma shouted across the paddock. Sheltie stood there, flicking his tail as he munched the carrot.

Emma had heard that a new family had moved into Fox Hall Manor on the other side of the orchard. The Armstrongs had gone to live in the city.

Mom had said that the new people had a little girl. A little girl about the same age as Emma. The mailman had seen her when the movers were unloading the moving truck the day before.

Emma was looking forward to making a

new friend. She wanted Sheltie to look his very best. That was why she had been trying to braid his tail.

But Sheltie thought it was a game and wouldn't keep still. In the end, Emma gave up and left his tail just as it was: long, straggly, and almost touching the ground.

Emma put on Sheltie's saddle and bridle, then rode him up the road toward Fox Hall Manor. They passed Mr. Crock's house, then crossed the little stream by the bridge at the end of the road. The road curved around open fields and the orchard until it almost met the woods at the back of Mr. Brown's meadow.

There, a long gravel drive wound its way up to a high wall with heavy iron gates. The gates were closed.

Emma rode right up and peered through the gates into the grounds of the manor.

Fox Hall was a grand place. The gardens were beautiful, with lawns and trees and flower beds planted like those in a park. The gravel drive led from the iron gates up through the gardens to the front door.

The place looked deserted. Emma couldn't see any sign of the new people. She looked very hard, peering through the gates. Sheltie looked, too. He pushed his nose through the bars and sniffed at the air. Sheltie could smell another pony.

Just then, Emma heard the sound of a car racing up the gravel drive behind them. When the driver slammed on the brakes to stop, the little car skidded sideways on the loose gravel and ended up with its back wheel stuck in a shallow, muddy pothole.

The car door flew open and a very red-faced man jumped out. He looked at the wheel stuck in the mud, then gave the tire a hard kick. He was in a very bad mood.

The man glanced over at Emma. He looked very grumpy.

"I thought you were Sally, my daughter," he said. "I thought she was outside the gates on her pony. That's not allowed!"

"Oh!" said Emma. "I'm not Sally. My name's Emma, and this is Sheltie."

"I know you're not Sally, you silly girl. For a moment I just thought you looked like her." He really was a grump. "And look what you've made me do!" he said. The man looked at his car again, and stood with his hands on his hips.

Emma didn't think the accident was her fault, but she decided it would be rude to say so.

"If you have a rope," said Emma, "Sheltie can pull your car out of that hole."

The man looked Sheltie up and down.

"What, that little thing?" he said. "He

doesn't look big enough to pull a baby's stroller."

"Sheltie may be small," said Emma. "But he's very strong. If you have a rope we'll show you."

The man had a rope in the trunk of the car. Emma dismounted and tied one end of the rope to the front of the car. Then she tied the other end around Sheltie's chest.

"Come on, Sheltie," whispered Emma. "We'll show him!"

The man started the engine. Sheltie pulled. Emma held on to his reins and Sheltie pulled as hard as he could.

The car moved, just an inch or so at first. And then, as Sheltie pulled harder, the back wheel came right up out of the pothole.

The man quickly unlocked the gates, then pulled the rope free and jumped back into the car. "Stand clear!" he shouted. Then he drove the car through and closed the gates behind him.

Emma stood with Sheltie on the other side of the gates. The man hadn't even stopped to say thank you. He was very rude.

As the man drove off up the driveway, Emma saw a girl come out of the house.

She stood on the front steps and looked down toward the gates. Emma gave a friendly wave, and the girl waved back.

Then the car pulled up at the house, and the man got out and led the girl back inside.

"That must have been Sally," said Emma. Sheltie's ears pricked up. "She

looked nice, didn't she?"

Sheltie gave a loud blow and sniffed at the air—Sheltie was more interested in the new pony he could smell.

Chapter Two

Back at home Emma told Mom all about the rude and grumpy man.

"You mustn't call him names, Emma," said Mom. "That must have been Mr. Jones. He was probably very worried if he thought Sally was locked out of the grounds."

"He didn't say she was *locked* out,"

said Emma. "He said she wasn't allowed to *be* out."

"Well, they did only move in yesterday," said Mom. "Perhaps he was afraid that Sally might wander off and get lost."

"You can't get lost in Little Applewood!" laughed Emma. And Mom agreed.

Later that afternoon, Emma and Sheltie were practicing their jumping in the paddock. Dad had rolled an old wooden barrel out into the paddock, and Emma wanted to jump Sheltie over it.

The wooden barrel was only two feet high. Sheltie flew over it like a bird. Emma was sure he could have jumped over six barrels. Well, maybe two!

Emma pretended she was a champion show jumper just like the ones she had seen on TV. She concentrated very hard and took Sheltie over the barrel again and again.

"Great job, Sheltie." Emma leaned forward and gave him a good pat. "You're fantastic."

Sheltie gave a loud snort and looked very pleased with himself.

Emma kept thinking about the new family that had moved into Fox Hall Manor. She wished that she had been able to meet Sally and say hello properly. But Emma thought it would be very difficult to make friends if Mr. Jones was around.

Emma asked Sheltie what he thought.

Sheltie shook his mane and flicked his long, straggly tail. Sheltie knew there was a pony hidden away up at the manor and, like Emma, he was looking forward to making a new friend. He became frisky just thinking about it.

Emma decided to make another visit to Fox Hall Manor. It would be at least another hour before lunch was ready. There was plenty of time to ride down the road and around the back meadow to the manor house.

They skirted the woods and soon came to the gravel drive.

Emma sat on Sheltie outside the big gates and peered through the bars into the grounds. There was no sign of Sally, or anyone else. It was a very big house for just three people to live in, thought Emma. There must be at least twenty rooms.

As Emma sat there, counting the windows, Sally came around the side of the house, riding a pony. A lovely black and white pony with a long, white mane. Sally saw Emma standing by the gate and immediately came trotting over.

"Hello," she said. "My name's Sally and this is Minnow."

Sheltie held his head high, gave a snort, and flicked his tail.

Sheltie was very interested in Minnow. He poked his nose through the gates and rubbed muzzles with the black and white pony.

"This is Sheltie, and I'm Emma."

The two girls smiled at each other. They were both about the same age and both had blonde hair, although Sally's was much longer than Emma's and was tied in a braid.

The two girls liked each other right
away.

"Sheltie looks very sweet," said Sally. "I
bet you have lots of fun with him." Sally
reached through the gate and stroked
Sheltie's nose. His eyes twinkled beneath his
bushy bangs and he gave a friendly snort.

"Minnow looks nice, too," said Emma. "I bet you have just as much fun when you're out riding!"

Sally shook her head.

"Minnow's a terrific pony, but I'm not allowed to ride him outside. My father says we have to stay inside the manor grounds."

"But once you know your way around Little Applewood, you'll be able to come out riding, won't you?" asked Emma. "I'll show you all the bridle paths so you won't get lost."

"I don't think so," said Sally. "It was the same in the old house. Daddy would never let me ride outside in case Minnow ran off or I had an accident."

"But Minnow looks like such a quiet

pony," said Emma. "I can't imagine him running off."

"That's what I think, too! But Daddy has a friend whose little girl was badly hurt in a riding accident. So he doesn't want me to ride outside. You can come and ride inside, though," added Sally. "At least I think you can. I'll have to ask first. Can you come back in the morning?"

Emma said she would. It was summer vacation, so she could come as often as Sally liked.

Emma watched Sally ride away across the grass. She wondered what Mr. Jones would say when Sally asked him. She hoped it would be all right.

On the way back home Emma passed Mr. Crock's house. Mr. Crock was sitting with Fred Berry on a little wooden bench outside in the garden. Emma gave the two men a friendly wave as she and Sheltie trotted by.

Emma remembered how unfriendly Mr.

Crock had been when they had first met. Things had changed since she'd gotten to know him better, and Emma hoped that maybe it would be the same with Mr. Jones.

They arrived back at the paddock just as Mom came out of the house to call Emma in for a snack. Emma was looking forward to telling Mom all about Sally and Minnow. And even more, she was looking forward to riding in the manor grounds tomorrow.

And so was Sheltie—Emma was certain.

☆ Chapter Three

The next morning Emma was really excited. She had breakfast early, gulping down her cereal. Then she fed Sheltie and put on his saddle, ready to go up the manor to visit Sally.

Emma told Sheltie to be on his best behavior. It was important that they made a good impression on Mr. Jones. After all, he hadn't been that friendly when they first met.

Sally was waiting with Minnow at the big gates. She was very pleased to see Emma.

"Mommy says it's okay if you and Sheltie come in," said Sally. "We can ride all morning. Daddy wasn't too pleased, but as long as we behave and don't go outside, he won't mind."

Sally jumped down from the saddle and pulled open the gates. Emma and Sheltie quickly hurried through and Sally closed the gates after them.

The grounds of Fox Hall Manor were like one huge garden that spread all around the big house. There were lawns and trees and even a pond with a statue in the middle. The statue was of a big swan standing with its wings spread out as though it were about to fly away. Water spouted from its open beak and trickled into the pond.

Emma noticed that wire netting had been fixed across the water. Sally said her father had fitted the netting in case of an accident.

Emma thought Mr. Jones was a bit funny. He always seemed to be worrying that something would happen to Sally. She wasn't allowed to ride outside or to have any fun. Emma thought it was very sad.

At the bottom of the grounds was a nice flat open meadow. Minnow had his stable down there. It was a proper wooden stable with doors and a cobblestone yard where

Sally could groom Minnow until his coat shined like satin. He already looked like a show pony.

Next to Minnow, Sheltie looked hairy and untidy with his long, straggly mane and tail. But Sheltie was a Shetland pony, and Emma liked the way he looked.

In the meadow, two jumps were set up. There were real pony jumps made of wood and brush. But they were very low, not even as high as Sheltie's barrel.

The two girls rode their ponies around and took the two jumps one after the other. Sheltie was showing off in front of Minnow and jumping much higher than he needed to.

Emma told Sally how she made her own jump with bricks and a plank of wood. Sheltie could jump six bricks high. Sally thought it sounded really wonderful.

Then Emma told Sally all about Little Applewood. She told Sally about Horseshoe Pond and the woods behind Prickly Forest. And when she told Sally about the rolling hills and the open countryside, Emma noticed a sad look on Sally's face.

"It must be lovely to ride out all on your own across the countryside," said Sally.

"It is," said Emma.

"I don't think I'll ever be allowed to ride outside," said Sally.

"Well, maybe one day," said Emma.

She was glad her mom and dad were not like Mr. Jones, never letting her go any-where.

When it was time for Emma to go home she suddenly had an idea.

"Would your dad let you come over to our house for lunch?" said Emma.

Sally's face lit up with a big bright smile. "That would be wonderful," she said. "I'll have to wait for the right moment to ask. I would really like to come."

Emma hoped that Mr. Jones would say yes.

When Emma left, Sally stood with Minnow at the big gates and watched Emma ride away on Sheltie. Sheltie's tail was swishing from side to side and Minnow gave a little whimper. He didn't seem to want his new friend to go and neither did Sally. She decided to ask right there and then if she could go and visit Emma for lunch. Later that afternoon, Mrs. Jones telephoned from Fox Hall Manor and spoke to Emma's mom. Sally was allowed to come over for lunch the following day. Sally spoke to Emma on the telephone and sounded very excited.

She told Emma that it was the first time

she had ever been visiting on her own, and she was looking forward to it more than anything in the world. She felt like a real grownup.

In the morning, Emma told Sheltie that they were having a luncheon with Sally. She waggled a packet of peppermints in front of him.

"And you can have some of these if you behave."

Sheltie snatched the packet out of Emma's hand and stood there with it sticking out of his mouth.

"Don't you *dare*!" said Emma with a half laugh.

Sheltie dropped the mints. As Emma bent down to pick them up, Sheltie nudged her bottom with his muzzle and sent her flying. Then he galloped off and Emma chased him all around the paddock.

★ ★ ★ ★ ★ ★ ★ ★

Mr. Jones brought Sally over for lunch at one o'clock on the dot. He kissed Sally good-bye and said he would be back at four to collect her.

Emma's mom told him not to worry and said she would take good care of Sally. They all stood and waved as Mr. Jones drove off back down the road.

It was a lovely sunny day, so Mom put a little table outside in the yard down by the paddock. Sheltie stood with his fuzzy chin resting on the top bar of the wooden fence, looking at all the sandwiches and little cakes. He knew that if he stood there watching long enough, Emma would give

him a piece of carrot cake, and maybe a peppermint or two. Sheltie loved his peppermints.

Little Joshua and Mom sat at the table with Emma and Sally. It was so nice sitting out in the yard, and Sheltie entertained them with his clowning.

First Sheltie galloped around in circles. Then he rolled over on the grass kicking his legs up in the air as he lay on his back.

And when he stood there and curled back his lips, showing two grinning rows of teeth, Sally laughed so much that she fell off her chair.

"I think Sheltie deserves a tidbit," said Mom. Joshua clapped his hands with glee.

Emma let Sally feed Sheltie a peppermint as a special treat.

While Sheltie was crunching away Emma asked Sally if she would like a ride.

⭐ Chapter Four

The two girls saddled up Sheltie and put on
his bridle. Sheltie was smaller than
Minnow, but Sally rode him beautifully.
Sheltie was enjoying himself, and when
Emma suggested a jump or two, his ears
pricked up like a rabbit's.

Emma made the jump with bricks and
the plank of wood. Six bricks high was

easy for Sheltie now, so she made it eight. Then she rolled the wooden barrel out of the stable to make a little course for two jumps.

Sally rode Sheltie once around the paddock, then took the first jump. After a short canter they went over the barrel. Everyone clapped and Sally blushed with pride.

"Do it again!" called Emma. Sally looked like a proper horsewoman. She really was a good little rider.

Sally took the jumps again. But as she circled the paddock to jump for a third time, she didn't see her father's car rolling down the road and into the drive.

One . . . two! Sheltie cleared the jumps just as Mr. Jones leaped out of the car.

"Sally!" he shouted at the top of his lungs.

The loud noise surprised everyone and made them jump. Sheltie gave an unexpected hop and Sally slid sideways off the saddle. Sheltie stood still as Sally lay on the soft grass. She was unhurt.

Mr. Jones came racing across to the paddock gate. He flung it open and ran to Sally. Emma got there first though and helped Sally up. Sally was perfectly all right, but Mr. Jones was shouting and making a terrible fuss.

"I knew something like this would happen!" he said. "I should never have let you come, Sally. You could have been killed!" He turned to Emma's mom. His face was red and very angry.

"I thought you were going to look after her," he said. "I should have known better!" Then he took Sally's hand and led her quickly to the car.

Poor Sally started to cry and Sheltie, who thought he had done something terribly wrong, made a bolt for the open gate and ran off.

"Sheltie," called Emma. "Come back!" But Sheltie was gone, trotting down the road.

Emma's mom followed Mr. Jones to the car. "Really, Mr. Jones," she said, "there's no need to get upset. Sally has been having a lovely time. And there's no harm done."

"Bah!" said Mr. Jones. Then he slammed the car door shut and drove off.

Emma raced down the road after

Sheltie. She found him waiting in Mr. Brown's meadow, hidden behind a bush.

"Come on, boy," said Emma. "It's all right. It wasn't your fault." She rode Sheltie back to the paddock.

"Oh dear," said Mom. "What a shame. Sally was having such a nice time as well!"

Emma's mom telephoned Fox Hall Manor and spoke to Mrs. Jones, who said Sally was very upset and Mr. Jones had made her go to her room. But Mrs. Jones was very nice and told Emma's mom not to worry. Her husband would calm down and everything would be all right in the morning. He always fussed over Sally and was a real worrier. She was sorry that Sally's visit had ended the way it did.

That night, Emma thought about Sally a lot. She decided to write her new friend a letter and take it over in the morning. There was a mailbox in the big gates and Sally would be able to read it and cheer herself up. Emma thought it would be nice if Sally knew that she had a friend who was thinking about her.

☆ Chapter Five

In the morning, after breakfast, whe
Emma and Sheltie rode up to the mano
they found the gates wide open. There wa
no sign of Sally anywhere. Emma poppe
the letter into the box just as Mr. Jone
came out of the house.

He saw Emma and Sheltie standing b
the gates and came racing down the drive

Mrs. Jones followed right behind him.

"It's all your fault!" Mr. Jones shouted at Emma. "Sally's taken Minnow and run away. And it's all your fault, putting silly ideas of adventure into her head. My little girl's run away from home."

Mrs. Jones caught hold of her husband's arm.

"Don't say such things, Bernard," she said. "It's not Emma's fault at all. If it's anyone's fault then it's our own. Keeping Sally in all the time has made her run off, *not* Emma and Sheltie."

Mr. Jones calmed down a bit.

"But she's gone all the same. Sally's run away. Do you have any idea where she may have gone, Emma?" His voice sounded all croaky, as though he was about to burst into tears.

Emma shook her head. "I'm sorry," she said. "I don't know where she could be. Perhaps she just went out for a little ride on her own. She told me she wanted to do that."

"No, she's gone!" snapped Mr. Jones. "She left a note saying that she has run away and is never coming back."

Sheltie put his head down. He didn't like it when people shouted.

"Maybe Sheltie and I can find Sally," said Emma. "We can go and look. We know all the bridle paths across the countryside and all around Little Applewood."

"I can't see how your stupid pony can find my little girl," said Mr. Jones. "It's a job for the police. I telephoned them half

an hour ago. If anyone's going to find her it will be the police!"

Suddenly, Mrs. Jones began crying. "Oh, Bernard," she said. "Let Emma go and look if she wants to. Sally is out there somewhere all on her own. We can't do anything here except wait."

Mr. Jones put his arm around his wife's shoulders and led her back inside the house. They were both very upset.

"Come on, Sheltie," said Emma. "Let's try and find Sally and Minnow."

Sheltie pricked his ears up and gave a loud blow. He seemed to understand everything that Emma said.

☆ Chapter Six

Emma squeezed her heels and Sheltie took off at a gallop. They raced down the lane to the woods behind Mr. Brown's meadow. If Sally had run away, thought Emma, she would probably be heading for the open countryside, through the woods.

Emma and Sheltie took the path they always rode to the woods, the one that skirted the meadow. Emma kept a lookout for any pony tracks. Sheltie sniffed at the air, trying to pick up Minnow's scent.

The ground was hard, and Emma could see no marks to show that Sally and Minnow had passed that way.

Emma and Sheltie pressed on until they came to the edge of Bramble Wood. There were several paths which led through the tangle of trees.

Sheltie pawed at the ground with his hoof and tossed his head. He wanted to take the long path which led up to higher ground. From there you could look out over the hills and down across Little Applewood. The path went up over the hills toward the main road and led on to the rolling meadow.

Emma and Sheltie rode through the woods beneath the overhanging trees. At some points, the branches hung so low that Emma had to brush them out of the way with her hand.

There was no sign of Sally, though, until they neared the edge of the wood where the path began to rise up to higher ground.

On a branch sticking out across the path, clinging to a twig, was a clump of white horse hair. Sheltie saw it first. He stopped dead in his tracks and sniffed at the coarse hair.

It was from Minnow's mane. Sheltie had no doubt about it. He recognized the scent right away. Sheltie gave a loud snort as Emma reached out with her hand and plucked the clump of hair free.

"Clever boy, Sheltie," said Emma. "They must have come this way after all." There were also a few hoofprints in the muddy track where the earth was softer.

Emma squeezed with her heels and hurried Sheltie along.

"Trot on, Sheltie!"

Sheltie quickened his pace to a trot. They rode out of the wood and climbed up to the top of the hill.

There weren't so many trees here. Emma could see for miles back down over Little Applewood and beyond, across to the rolling meadow. There was still no sign of Sally and Minnow.

"Which way, Sheltie?" said Emma.

Sheltie shook his long mane and sniffed the air through his nostrils. Minnow's scent was on the wind, but it was very faint.

Emma eased the reins and let Sheltie take the lead. He flicked his tail a couple of times. Then he set off over the grass across a shallow slope, heading for the meadow.

An old railway line used to run through the valley on the other side of the slope between the meadow and the hillside. Emma could see where the railway tracks had been. The grass was thinner there and the ground was stony with gravel and rocks.

Emma and Sheltie followed the tracks until they disappeared into an abandoned tunnel that cut into the hillside. Sheltie stopped at the entrance to the tunnel and peered inside. A wooden barrier lay across the opening, warning people to keep out. Sheltie made funny little snorting sounds and pawed at the ground with his hoof.

"Is it them, Sheltie?" said Emma. "Are

Sally and Minnow in there?"

Sheltie nodded his head and gave a loud blow.

"Sally," Emma called into the tunnel. "Are you in there?"

Emma's voice echoed back from inside the tunnel.

Are you in there . . . there . . . there. The echo faded to silence. Then Emma heard someone calling. A little voice sounding far away.

"Help!"

Sheltie heard it, too. His ears stood straight up.

"Sally, is that you?" Emma called again. And this time she recognized Sally's voice.

"Help! I'm in here!"

It was very dark inside the tunnel. But Emma knew Sally was in trouble, so she urged Sheltie forward.

Slowly they edged their way around the barrier and into the darkness. Sheltie had to be very careful. The ground was uneven

where the railway tracks had been removed, and there were dips and holes everywhere. Farther into the tunnel, the floor became wet and slippery.

Emma saw a faint light up ahead. It was

Sally. She was walking back along the tunnel toward Emma with a flashlight. Sally carried a small backpack and her clothes looked all wet and muddy. Emma could see that Sally had been crying. Her cheeks were wet with tears.

"Sally!" called Emma.

Sally ran the last few feet to meet her friend. Emma jumped down from the saddle and gave poor Sally a big hug.

"Oh, Emma," cried Sally, "I'm so glad to see you! It's Minnow. He's fallen down and trapped his leg. And it's all my fault." She began to cry again.

Chapter Seven

Sally told Emma how the ground suddenly sloped away down into a big dip up ahead. There was a hole where some old railway ties were stacked. Minnow had missed his footing and fallen into it. His leg was trapped by one of the wooden rails, and he couldn't move. They could hear poor Minnow up ahead in the darkness, whimpering and making sad whinnying noises.

"We've got to help him," said Sally. "We've got to get Minnow out. I'll never run away again, I promise. I only wanted to ride out on my own like you and Sheltie, Emma. I never meant to put Minnow in danger."

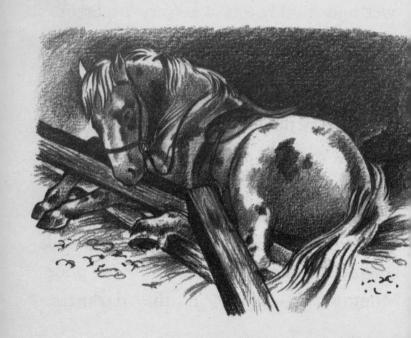

Emma held Sally's hand and led Sheltie along in the dark to where Minnow was trapped. Sally shined her flashlight and they could see the little black and white pony lying on his side in the hole, unable to get up.

Minnow's lovely white mane was all wet and muddy. He was very frightened. When Minnow saw Sheltie, he calmed down a little and gave a friendly blow.

Emma climbed down the slope into the hole. The wooden rail was very heavy. As hard as Emma tried, she couldn't move it. Minnow's leg was truly stuck.

"We need a rope," said Emma. "Then maybe Sheltie could help and pull the rail away."

"But we haven't got a rope," said Sally.

Emma thought about it for a while. Then she had an idea.

"We can use Minnow's reins," she said. "And I've got a belt. We can use the straps on your backpack and tie them all together."

It was a brilliant idea, and the two girls set to work without a moment to lose.

Sally climbed down to Minnow and carefully slipped the reins off over the little pony's head. Emma unclipped the two straps from Sally's backpack and took off the belt from her jeans.

When they tied them all together, they had a strong line. It was long enough to fix around one end of the wooden rail that trapped Minnow's leg. The other end was tied to Sheltie's girth.

Emma turned Sheltie around. They were ready to give it a try.

Emma gave Sheltie a hug and whispered in his ear. "It's up to you, Sheltie. I know you can do it."

She led Sheltie forward and the line took the strain. Sheltie pulled as hard as he could. The wooden rail moved a little bit, but not enough to free Minnow's leg. A second rail was stopping the first from moving any farther.

Sheltie tried again, but it was no good. Each time Sheltie pulled, the second rail

seemed to stick even more.

"We can't give up," said Sally. "We've got to get Minnow out."

Sheltie stood with his head cocked to one side. Sally shined her flashlight into the hole, and Sheltie looked at the problem.

Very slowly, Sheltie started to move forward. Carefully, he picked his way over the rails and went down into the hole. Minnow raised his head and the two ponies nuzzled noses. Then Sheltie bent his head low and began to push the second rail with his nose.

Sheltie had a thick neck and was very strong. The rail moved a little bit. Then Sheltie pushed again and nudged it to one side. One final push and the rail came free and rolled away. Minnow snorted.

Sheltie scrambled back up out of the hole and gave a loud snort. He was ready to try again and pull the other rail away.

Emma turned Sheltie around and led him forward again. This time the thick wooden rail moved easily.

As soon as Sheltie had dragged it free, Sally jumped down into the hole and helped Minnow up onto his feet. The little rescued pony was so happy to scramble out of the hole that he rushed up to Sheltie and gave a loud blow to his ear.

Emma clapped her hands with joy. The two girls untied the straps and reins, then unfastened the belt from Sheltie's girth. Sally put Minnow's reins back on to the bridle and put her backpack together. As Emma buckled up her belt, the two girls looked at each other with big smiles. They had done it! Or rather, Sheltie had.

Sally gave Sheltie a good hard pat. She ruffled his mane and planted a big kiss on his nose. Then she and Emma led the two ponies back along the tunnel.

Chapter Eight

"We must be very careful," said Emma. "There are still a lot of holes up ahead."

They walked very slowly, one pony behind the other, with Sheltie leading the way. They could see the light at the end of the tunnel. Soon they were all standing outside in the bright sunshine.

Minnow was limping slightly. His leg

was scraped and very sore. "He's going to have a nasty bruise there," said Emma. "You'll need to get the vet to come over and look at him, Sally."

As they made their way back over the hill and along the woodland path, Sally looked worried.

"Daddy will be very cross," she said. "what with me running away and everything. And now Minnow's hurt. He's going to be *so* angry. I bet he won't let me ride Minnow ever again!"

Sally suddenly looked very sad.

"Don't be silly," said Emma. "He's going to be so pleased to see you safe and sound, he probably won't say anything."

"Oh yes he will," said Sally. "You don't know him. It was wrong to run away like that, but I just had to ride Minnow out on my own. What's the use of having a pony if you're not allowed to ride him!"

"Perhaps he'll understand if you explain," said Emma.

"I hope so," said Sally, but she knew he wouldn't.

They finally came out of the wood and took the curving path which skirted the meadow and led to Fox Hall Manor. Sally was shaking with nerves.

The big manor house loomed up in front of them. Emma and Sally walked with the ponies side by side. Minnow was still limping as they went through the open gates and up to the house.

Suddenly the front door blew open, and Mr. Jones came rushing out. Mrs. Jones was right behind him. Her eyes were red from crying.

"Sally!" Mr. Jones called out at the top of his voice. "Where have you been?" He ran up to Sally and swept her up in his arms, pushing past Emma and accidentally knocking her off balance. Emma sat down with a bump.

Mrs. Jones helped Emma up onto her feet.

"Thank heavens you're safe. Where on earth have you been? Why did you run off like that?"

Sally couldn't find her voice. She didn't say a thing.

"Sally only wanted to ride out on her own," began Emma.

Mr. Jones looked at her crossly. He was very angry.

"And what are *you* doing here?" he snapped. "Go home! You've caused enough trouble for one day. This is all your fault. I never want to see you around here again!" Then he turned away and carried Sally up to the house.

Poor Emma was near tears. Mrs. Jones took Minnow's rein and put a friendly hand on Emma's shoulders.

"I'm sorry about my husband, Emma," said Mrs. Jones. "Don't take any notice. He's very upset. The police have been out for hours looking for Sally. I can't thank you enough for finding her and bringing her home. None of this is your fault, Emma."

Emma swallowed back her tears. "It was Sheltie, really," she said. "Sheltie found Sally and Minnow. And he got Minnow out of the hole."

Mrs. Jones didn't know anything about the tunnel and how Minnow was trapped, but she suddenly noticed the pony's injured leg.

"I think you should call the vet," said Emma. "Minnow's leg needs looking after."

"Thank you, Emma. I'll telephone him right away. Now you go home. Your mother will be getting worried." She thanked Emma again, then led Minnow off to his stable.

Emma and Sheltie watched her go, then closed the gates behind them and went home.

★ ★ ★ ★ ★ ★ ★ ★

"You're just in time to help me set out the plates for lunch," said Mom. She popped a casserole into the oven and took some knives and forks from the kitchen drawer.

When Emma didn't say anything, Mom noticed that she was upset. Something was wrong. Even little Joshua could tell that Emma was unhappy. He stopped scribbling in his drawing book and looked up.

"What's the matter, Emma?" asked Mom.

Emma told her everything that had happened. How Sally had run away and how Sheltie had led the way to the old railway tunnel where Minnow was trapped.

Mom listened carefully as Emma

described how clever Sheltie had been and how they had made a line and rescued the little pony.

When she told Mom how cross Mr. Jones had been, Mom understood why Emma was so upset.

"Oh dear, Emma. It must have been awful. But it wasn't your fault. Mr. Jones must have been terribly worried anyway. You were very brave and clever to find Sally and Minnow like that. Good old Sheltie. It's a good thing he's such a clever little pony."

"But Mr. Jones said I can't ever see Sally again. It's not fair!" Emma started to cry, and Mom gave her a hug.

"I expect he'll calm down now that Sally's safe and sound," said Mom. "Give him a day or two. I'm sure he'll come around. He's probably very sorry for all those things he said."

But Emma wondered if Mr. Jones ever would come around. He had looked so angry. Emma thought he would never forgive her for what had happened, even though it wasn't her fault at all.

Chapter Nine

All that afternoon, Emma kept thinking about poor Sally. She tried to imagine what it would be like if she could never ride Sheltie outside in the beautiful countryside. Emma felt very lucky, but very sad and sorry for Sally at the same time.

Emma spent the rest of the afternoon in the paddock with Sheltie. She kept herself

busy, cleaning out his field shelter and pol-
ishing his saddle and bridle.

Then she gave Sheltie a good brush and
groomed his tail and mane until it was time
to go in for a snack. Sheltie had never
looked so neat and tidy. He would never
look as smart as Minnow, but Emma loved
him the way he was.

After her snack, Emma thought about
riding over to Fox Hall Manor just to see if
she could catch a glimpse of Sally. But
Mom said it would be best to keep away
for a while and give Mr. Jones time to calm
down. Mom said that she would telephone
Mrs. Jones in the morning and ask after
Sally.

That evening Emma watched her
favorite program on television before she

went to bed, but all the time she kept thinking of poor Sally. At least she would be able to see Sally when she started school, she thought. That cheered her up.

Mr. Jones couldn't stop Sally from going to school.

In the morning, while Emma was out giving Sheltie his breakfast, Mom telephoned Mrs. Jones. Mom told Emma that Mr. Jones was coming over later to have a talk.

Emma was worried when she heard this, so Mom suggested that Emma take a picnic lunch up to Horseshoe Pond to keep out of the way. Emma didn't argue.

Mom made up a little basket of goodies, with sandwiches, chips, cookies, and a big bottle of lemonade. There was so much food in the basket Emma thought that she would never manage to eat it all on her own.

Sheltie was very interested in the picnic

basket. He could smell the sandwiches and cookies, and tried to pull out a packet of chips as Emma laid the basket down on the grass to saddle him up.

"Not yet, Sheltie. There will be plenty for you when we get to Horseshoe Pond," said Emma.

Sheltie could hardly wait. He became frisky and swished his tail with excitement.

They took the long way through the apple orchard and followed the little stream to the big meadow. Emma popped two apples into the basket for Sheltie.

"Wouldn't it have been nice, Sheltie, if Sally could have come with us?" said Emma. Sheltie twitched his ears and listened as Emma spoke.

Horseshoe Pond was as pretty as ever.

Emma sat on a little island to eat her lunch. Sheltie nibbled at the dandelions growing beneath the sycamore tree. Emma fed the ducks on the pond with one of the cakes from the picnic basket.

Suddenly, Sheltie looked up, bright and alert. His eyes shined through his long bangs as he sniffed the air.

Then Sheltie gave a loud snort and Emma looked around. Trotting across the meadow on Minnow was Sally!

Emma jumped up. She couldn't believe it. At first she thought Sally had run away again. But then she saw that Sally was laughing and smiling with a big grin. Sheltie did a funny little stomping dance and ran forward to greet Minnow.

"What are you doing here?" said

Emma. "You dad will go crazy!"

"No, he won't," laughed Sally as she leaped from her saddle. "I think everything's going to be all right after all. Mommy had a long talk with Daddy this morning. And now he's at the cottage talking with *your* mom and dad. He's finally

agreed to let me ride out on my own. Mommy says I'm old enough to keep out of trouble. Daddy didn't like the idea very much. But he said I can, as long as I promise not to go too far. Isn't it fantastic?"

Emma was so pleased.

"Did my mom send you over here?" asked Emma.

"Yes," laughed Sally. "She spoke to Mommy this morning and asked about the picnic."

Emma suddenly realized why there was so much food in the picnic basket. Her mom had known all along that Sally would be able to come. It was the best surprise ever.

The two girls sat beneath the sycamore tree and laid out all the sandwiches and cakes on the picnic cloth. Sheltie and Minnow nuzzled up to each other and stood quietly in the shade, nibbling grass.

From the little island, Emma pointed out to Sally all the best places to ride. Sally couldn't wait to explore. It was going to be

great living in Little Applewood and having Emma and Sheltie as her friends.

★   ★   ★   ★   ★   ★   ★   ★

A little while later, Mr. Jones came
walking by with Emma's mom and dad.
Joshua was riding piggyback on Dad's
shoulders.

Mr. Jones was smiling and Emma
thought he looked really nice. Much better
than the grumpy man he was before. He
apologized to Emma and told her how
sorry he was for being so rude.

"I've been very silly," he said. "Ever
since my friend's little girl was hurt, I've
worried about Sally being hurt, too. But
accidents can happen anywhere. And it
can't be much fun having a pony with
nowhere to ride it."

He really was very grateful to Emma and Sheltie for finding Sally and bringing her home safely.

"You're a very brave and clever girl,

Emma," said Mr. Jones. "And Sheltie must be the cleverest pony for miles around."

And with that, Sheltie snatched a packet of potato chips from Emma's hand and raced off across the meadow with Minnow giving chase.

Mr. Jones laughed with a loud bellow.

"I can see Sally's going to be in safe hands with friends like Emma and Sheltie to look out for her," he said.